Sofia and the Baby Bird

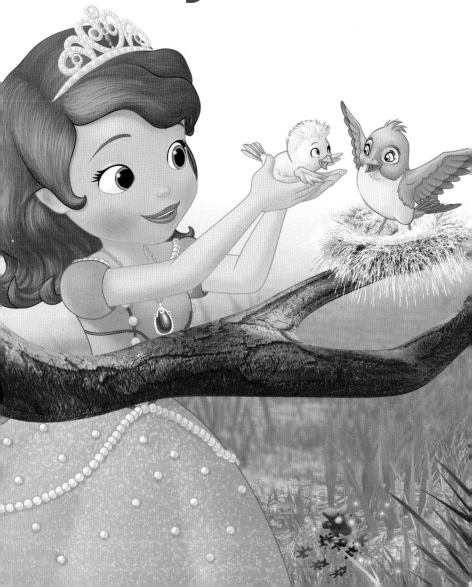

"Hello, baby bird!" says Sofia.

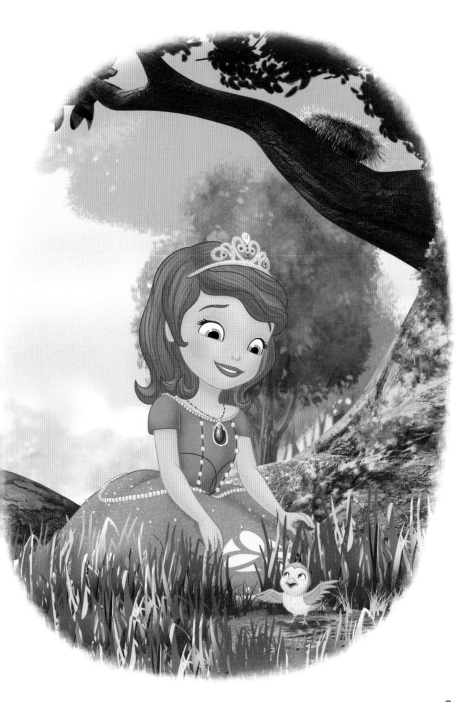

The baby bird eats.

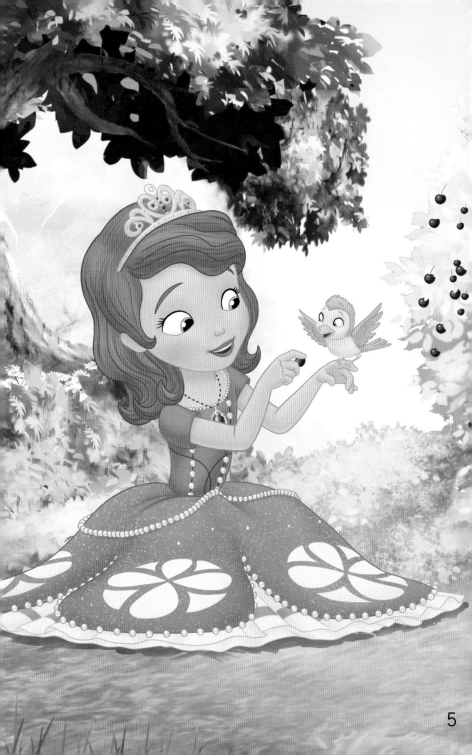

The baby bird sits.

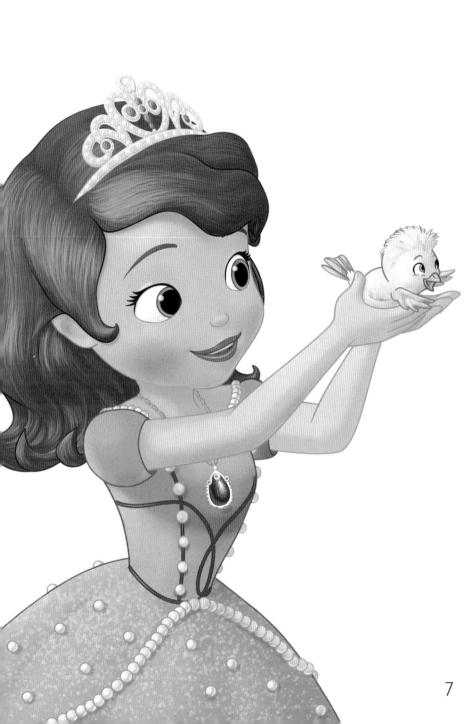

The baby bird sings.

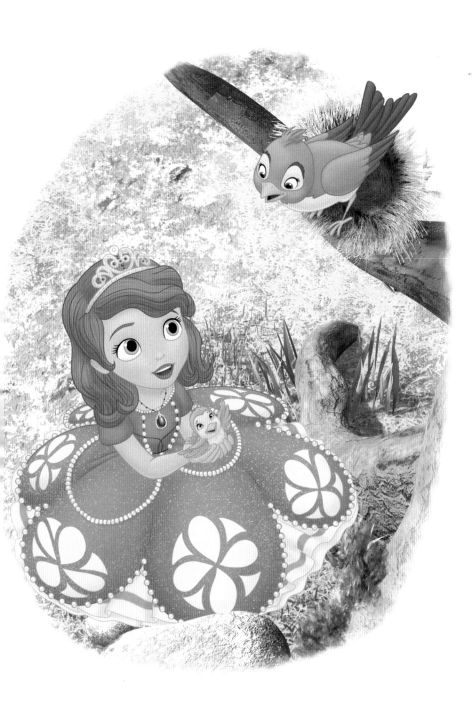

The baby bird stands.

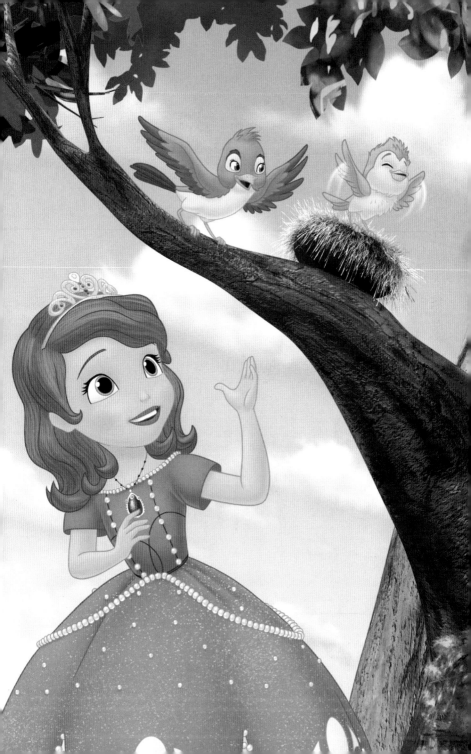

The baby bird flies!

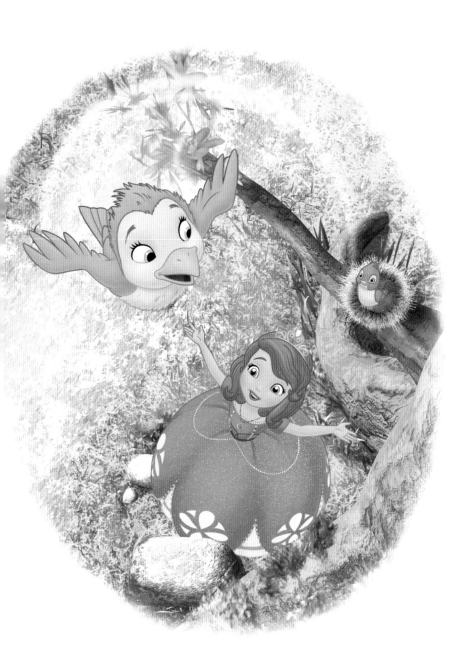

"Good-bye, baby bird!"
says Sofia.

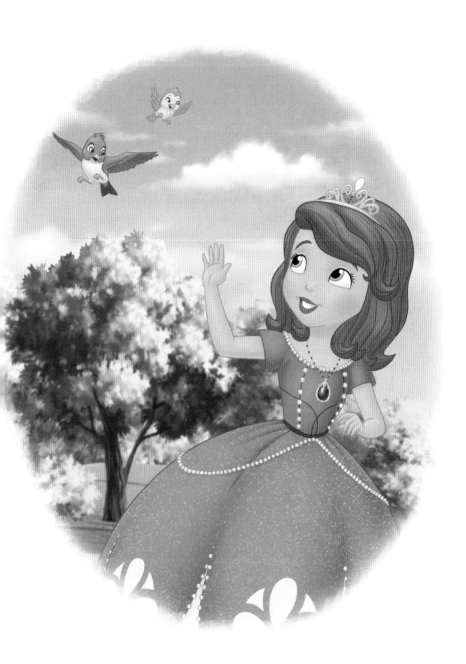

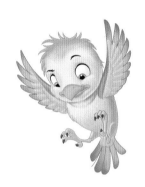